THE DARK KNIGHT RISES™

THE SECRET FILES

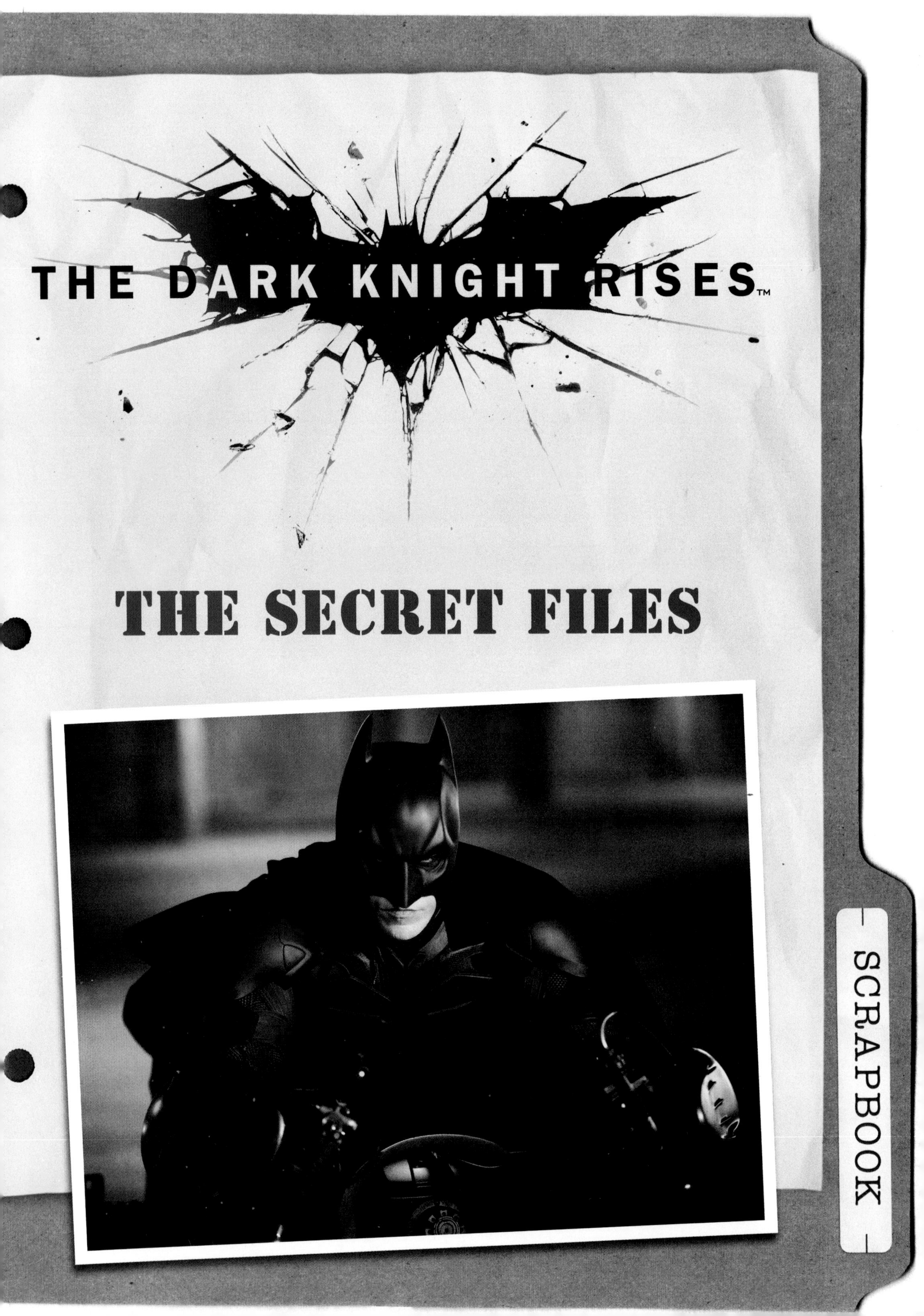

SCRAPBOOK

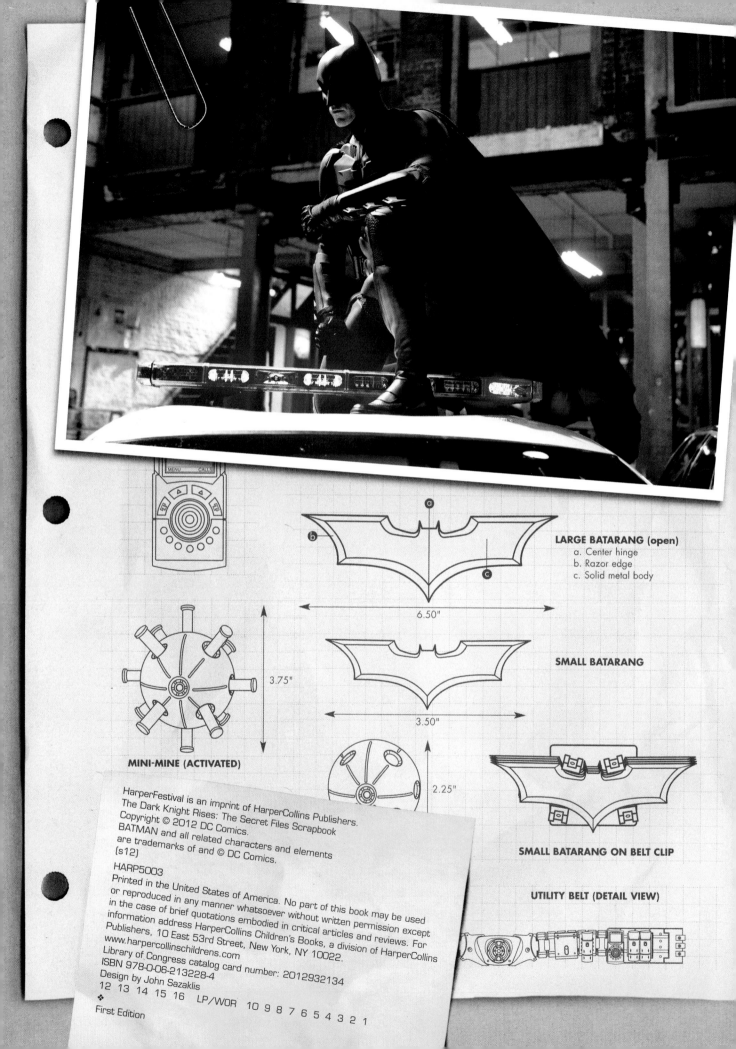

LARGE BATARANG (open)
a. Center hinge
b. Razor edge
c. Solid metal body

6.50"

SMALL BATARANG

3.50"

MINI-MINE (ACTIVATED)

3.75"

2.25"

SMALL BATARANG ON BELT CLIP

UTILITY BELT (DETAIL VIEW)

HarperFestival is an imprint of HarperCollins Publishers.
The Dark Knight Rises: The Secret Files Scrapbook
Copyright © 2012 DC Comics.
BATMAN and all related characters and elements
are trademarks of and © DC Comics.
(s12)

HARP5003
Printed in the United States of America. No part of this book may be used
or reproduced in any manner whatsoever without written permission except
in the case of brief quotations embodied in critical articles and reviews. For
information address HarperCollins Children's Books, a division of HarperCollins
Publishers, 10 East 53rd Street, New York, NY 10022.
www.harpercollinschildrens.com
Library of Congress catalog card number: 2012932134
ISBN 978-0-06-213228-4
Design by John Sazaklis
12 13 14 15 16   LP/WOR   10 9 8 7 6 5 4 3 2 1
❖
First Edition

THE DARK KNIGHT RISES™

THE SECRET FILES SCRAPBOOK

WRITTEN BY
BRANDON T. SNIDER

Inspired by the film
THE DARK KNIGHT RISES

Screenplay by
JONATHAN NOLAN and CHRISTOPHER NOLAN

Story by
CHRISTOPHER NOLAN and DAVID S. GOYER

BATMAN created by BOB KANE

HARPER FESTIVAL
An Imprint of HarperCollinsPublishers

When I was a small boy, a mugger shot and killed my parents. As an adult I pushed myself to the limits and trained to avenge their deaths and rid Gotham City of crime. After finding the perfect symbol to strike fear in the hearts of criminals I became Batman, the Dark Knight.

WAYNE MANOR

The original Wayne Manor had been around for more than a hundred and fifty years and was part of Gotham's historic legacy until it burned down. I later rebuilt the castle-like home to preserve my family's esteemed name. The manor's wealth and elegance serves to hide the secrets kept beneath it. During the Civil War, my great-grandfather used a secret passage hidden within the manor to usher slaves safely to freedom as part of the Underground Railroad. By playing a keystroke on the family piano, a doorway would open to reveal an old steel elevator shaft which led down and out through a cavern.

As a crime fighter I realized that I'd need a place to house my weapons and develop my detective skills. I found one deep below my home in the caves underneath Wayne Manor.

The Batcave serves as a hide-out. This is where I store my weapons and body armor. It's also where I use state-of-the-art technology to monitor criminal activity around Gotham.

THE CAVE ENTRANCE

There are only two entrances to the Batcave: through an elevator shaft hidden in Wayne Manor and through a secret cave entrance that is masked by a waterfall. Secrecy is very important to me, and the Wayne Manor grounds are closely monitored for suspicious activity. No one gets into the Batcave unannounced.

THE BAT-BUNKER

When I was forced out of my cave headquarters due to a devastating fire, I made a new base to be closer to downtown. It was there that the Bat-Bunker was born. During my time in the bunker, I installed a special hydraulic system that would hide my computers, printers, and other devices by lowering them into the floor.

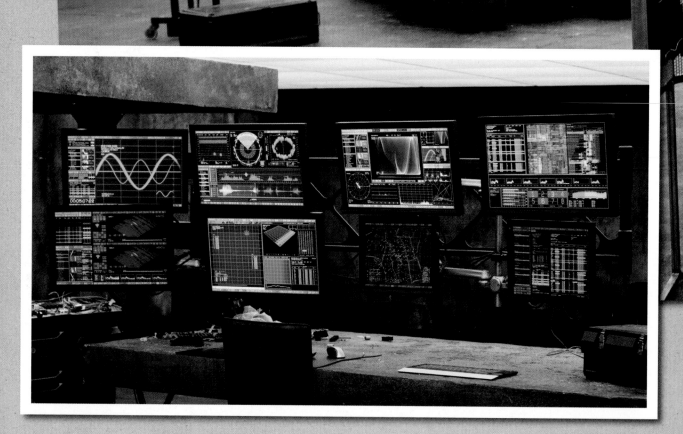

THE BATCOMPUTER

In order to monitor all criminal activities in Gotham effectively, an up-to-date and high-tech computer system was required. Thankfully, through Wayne Enterprises, I was able to buy the world's most advanced database and one of the largest mainframe computers. A monitor bay allows me to track television broadcasts and police radio bands while LCD screens track all the goings-on in Gotham.

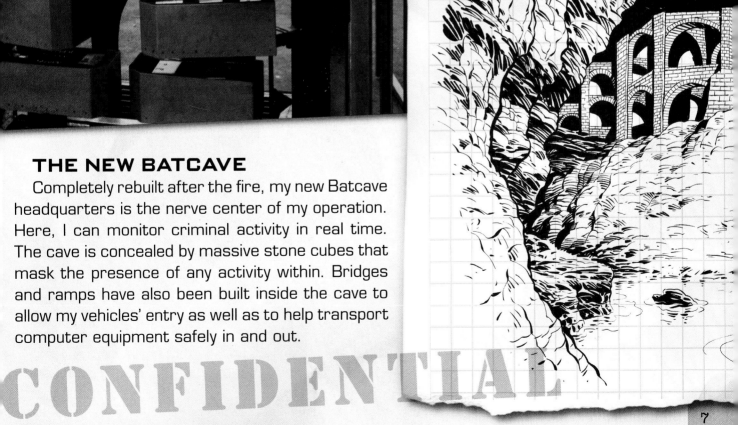

THE NEW BATCAVE

Completely rebuilt after the fire, my new Batcave headquarters is the nerve center of my operation. Here, I can monitor criminal activity in real time. The cave is concealed by massive stone cubes that mask the presence of any activity within. Bridges and ramps have also been built inside the cave to allow my vehicles' entry as well as to help transport computer equipment safely in and out.

CONFIDENTIAL

COWL

My cowl has a graphite exterior plated with Kevlar, a dense fiber plating that is bulletproof. My cowl acts as a helmet and protects my head during an attack. It is divided into two pieces, and it fastens around my neck.

UTILITY BELT

My Utility Belt allows me to carry weapons and gadgetry anywhere. I have throwing spikes, mini-mines, and Batarangs, as well as medical items and communication devices, at my disposal. My grapnel gun attaches to the front buckle of the belt and additional weapons can go on the back.

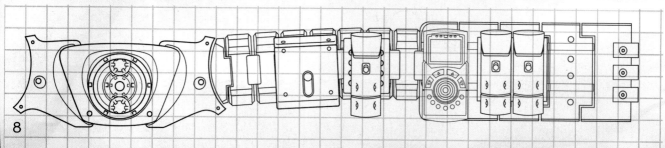

Radio circuitry inside my cowl allows me to monitor police bands as well as to eavesdrop on secret conversations. Filters in the nose act like a gas mask, and night vision lenses help me see clearly in the dark.

CAPE

My cape is made of memory cloth—a lightweight, fire-resistant fabric. The cape can hold different shapes when activated by controls in my gloves. Sometimes I use it as a glider or parachute. It gives me the ability to swoop down silently on my opponents.

AYNE ENTERPRISES
APPLIED SCIENCES DIVISION

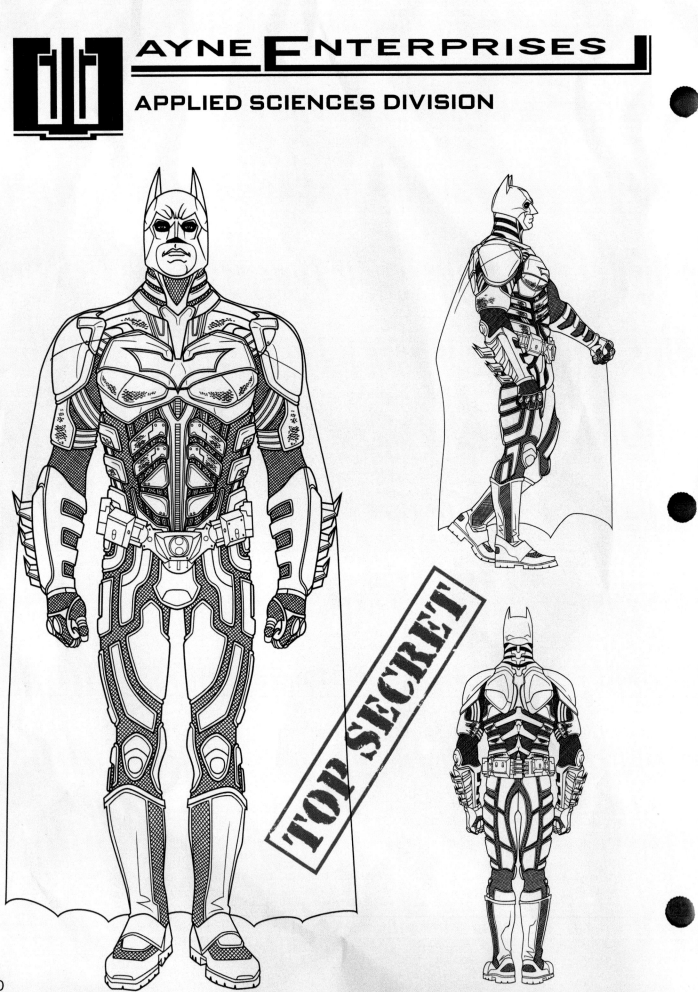

TOP SECRET

ARMOR

The Batsuit's armor is made of hardened bulletproof material and is impervious to most attacks. Each protective Kevlar plate is anchored to a thick elastic mesh that allows me to move freely. The armor is tear resistant and has reinforced joints. However, the absence of full-body plating leaves me vulnerable to attack in some places. The suit is fire resistant as well as invisible to infrared detection.

GAUNTLETS

My gauntlets are gloves braced with forearm shields that are primarily a defensive weapon for blocking attacks. For increased protection, the gauntlets have Kevlar plating. They also have a spring mechanism that fires blades like throwing stars.

GRAPNEL GUN

It's critical for me to be able to remove myself quickly from dangerous situations. In order to do this, I have a magnetic grapnel gun that uses a CO_2 canister to fire a thin climbing wire with a hooked end.

I keep the gun with me at all times on my Utility Belt.

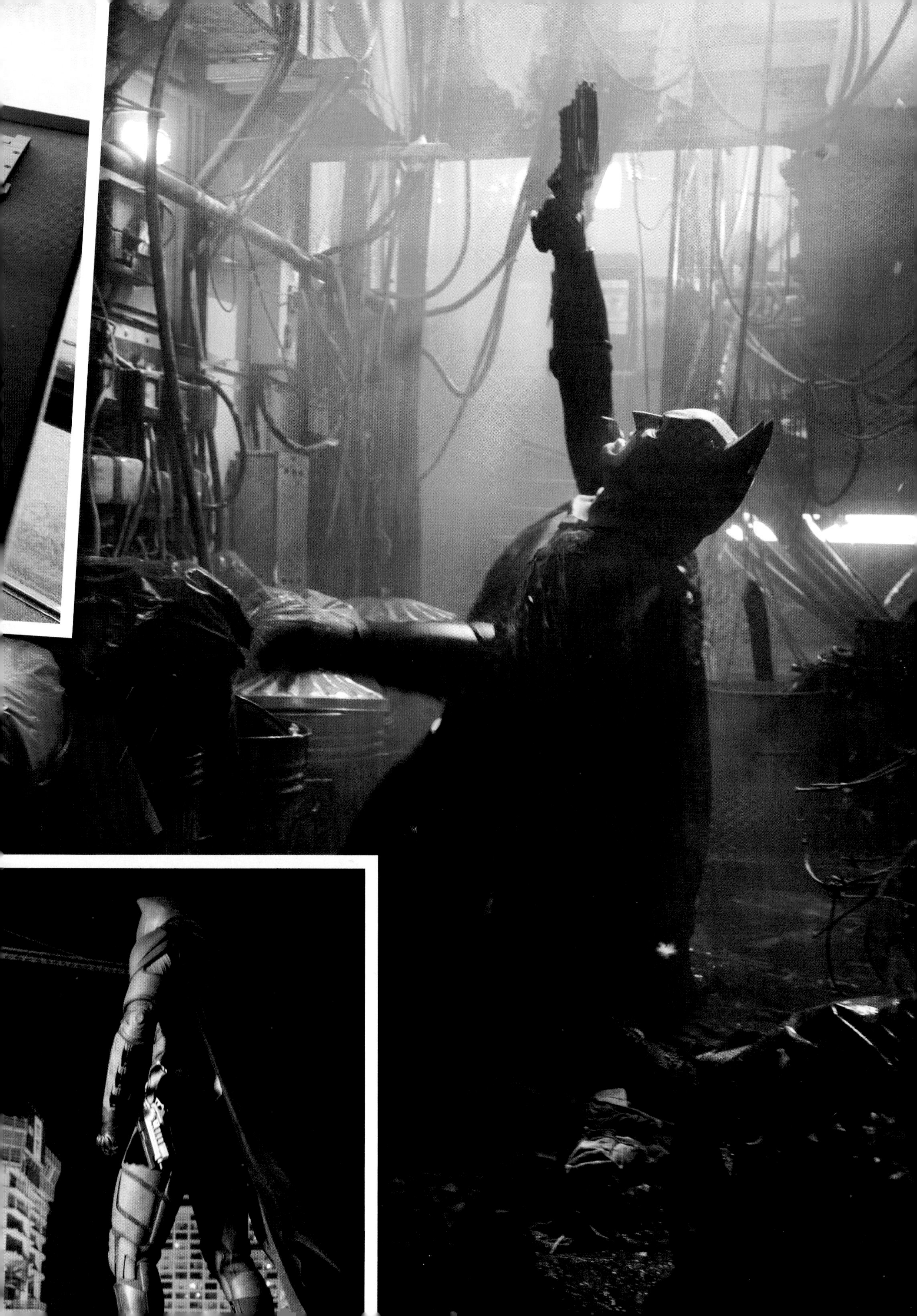

BATARANG

The Batarang is my weapon of first choice. It's like a boomerang, but it comes in many shapes and sizes and has a wide range of uses. Some have sharpened edges, some attach to cables to help me climb, some even emit smoke or sounds. I always keep a solid and a spring-loaded version in my Utility Belt.

SMOKE BOMBS & MINI-MINES

Smoke bombs are tiny circular devices that I use to create diversions to escape tricky situations. I also carry explosive thermite bombs, which are mini-mines that can blast through most doors and locks.

HANDHELD COMPUTER

Communication in the field is incredibly important. With my handheld computer, I'm able to contact my butler and trusted assistant Alfred quickly in the event of an emergency. The device also can relay commands to the Batmobile when I need to make a fast getaway.

MANGLER

The pneumatic mangler gives me the ability to bend or even cut through metal. With it, I can bend a rifle's shaft or destroy metal objects. The mangler is incredibly useful and attaches to the outside of my gauntlet.

STICKY BOMB GUN

The pump action, sticky bomb gun fires an explosive gummy compound that can stick to a variety of surfaces such as glass and concrete. The gun can be folded in half and stored on the back of the Utility Belt.

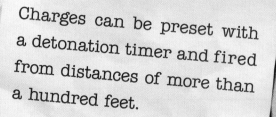

Charges can be preset with a detonation timer and fired from distances of more than a hundred feet.

EMP RIFLE

When fired, the EMP rifle releases a wave of electromagnetic energy that renders all electronic equipment in its range useless. The EMP rifle has attachments that allow it to fit onto both the Bat-Pod and the Bat.

CONFIDENTIAL

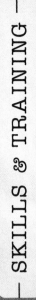

Even though I have some of the most advanced weapons in the world, it's crucial for me to take care of my mind and body. Jiujitsu and Ninjutsu training give me the stamina and focus I need. I've also learned the importance of studying my opponents for weaknesses and the need to be constantly aware of my surroundings.

My strength and vigilance help me stay one step ahead of the criminals I fight.

BATMOBILE

The Batmobile, also known as the Tumbler, was originally built to transport soldiers during wartime. Now I use it to travel within Gotham City limits. The Batmobile comes complete with the latest high-tech weapons and a stealth mode that makes it virtually undetectable.

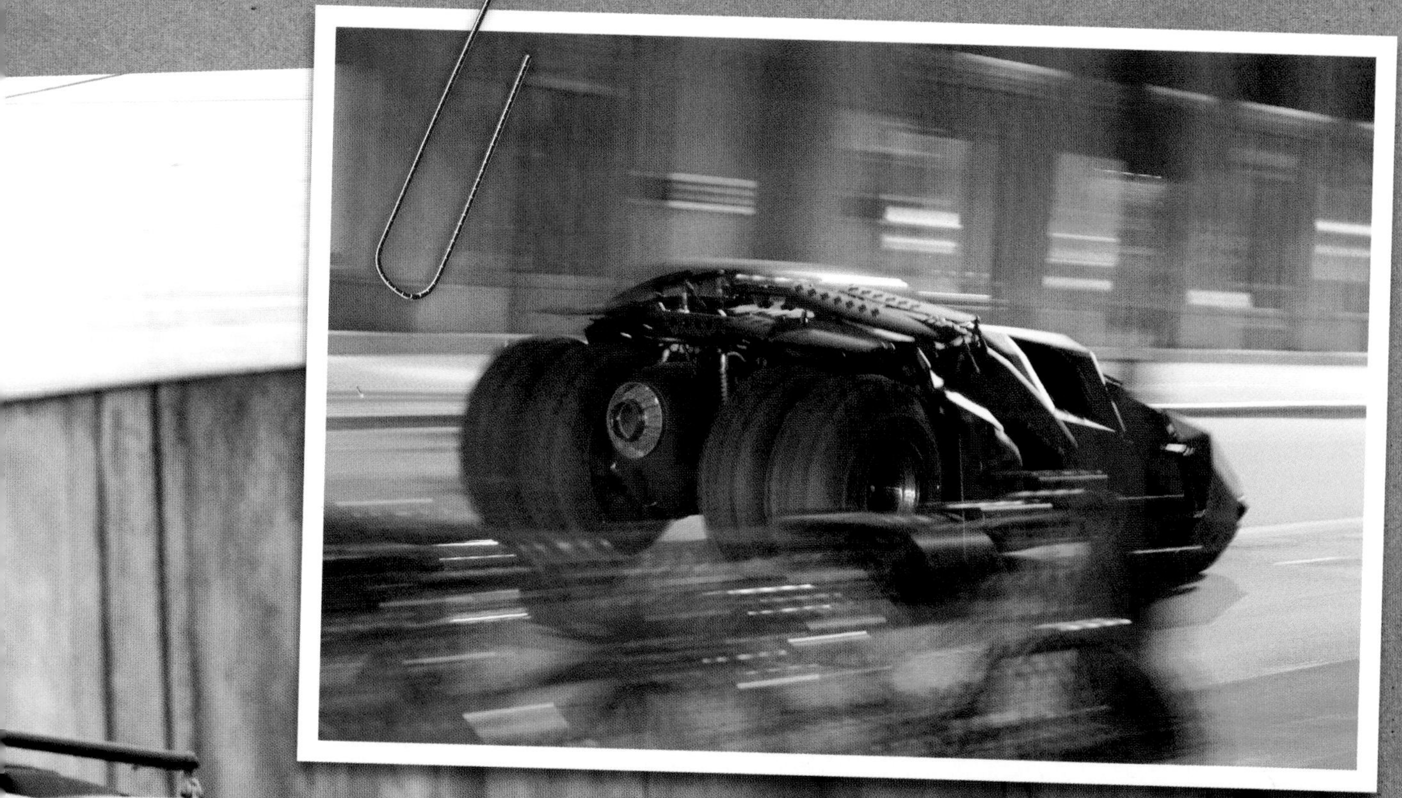

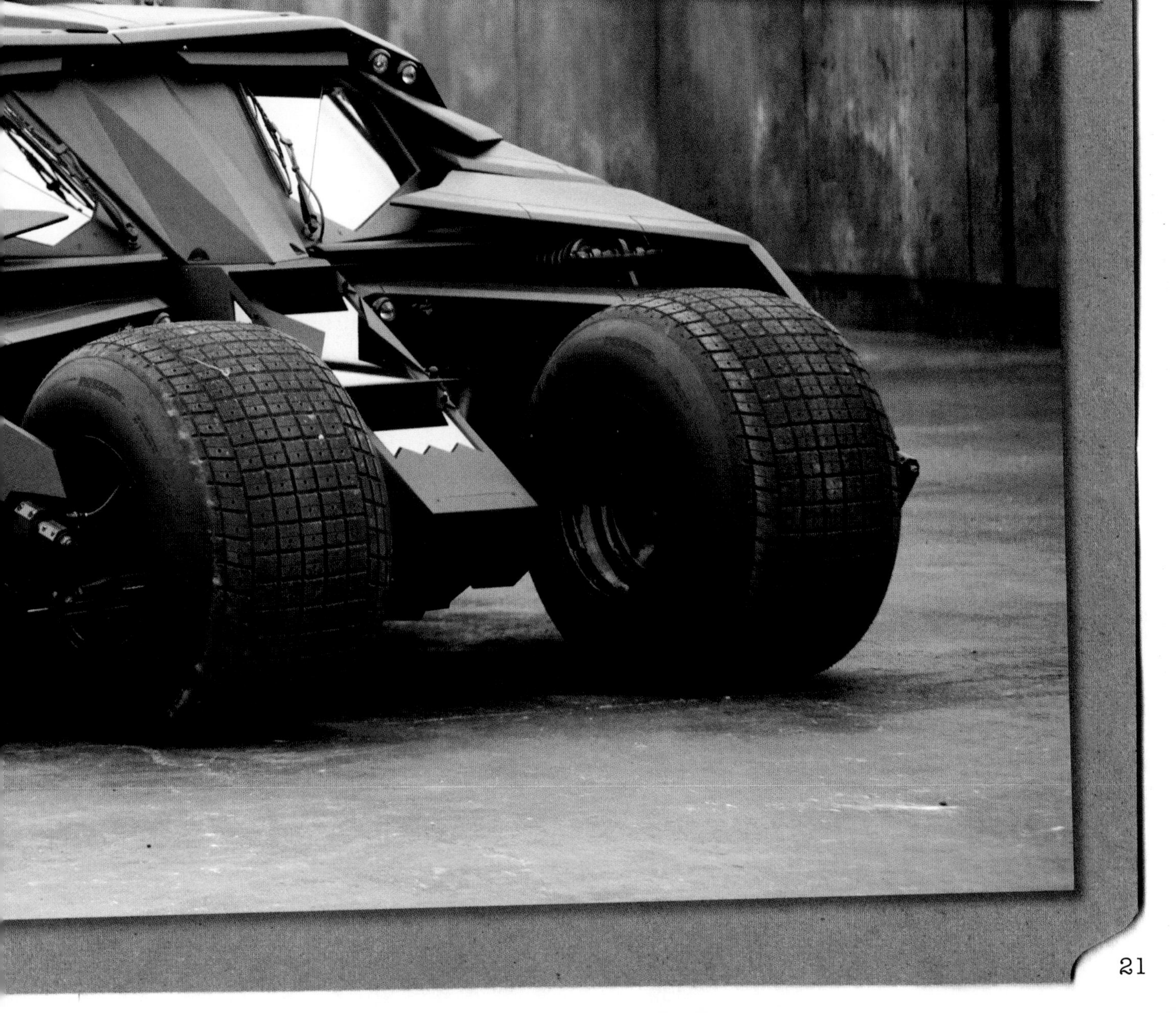

APPLIED SCIENCES DIVISION

SPECS

WEIGHT: 2.5 tons
LENGTH: 15 feet
WIDTH: 9 feet, 4 inches
HEIGHT: 5 feet, 2 inches
SPEED: 200+ mph,
   0–60 mph in 2.9 seconds

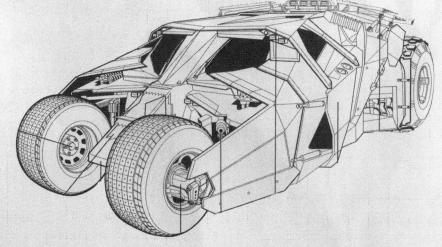

EXTERNAL DETAILS

Jet engine
Machine guns
Missile launchers
Protective blast shutters
Halogen spotlights
Thermal imaging DVE
  (driver's vision enhancement)
Forward, rear, and side hydraulic airfolds
Roof access canopy
Small protruding spikes for traction on unstable roadways
No front axle enables the Tumbler to make extremely tight turns
44" Super Swamper tires flank rear exhaust jet
2 drag chutes can deploy from the rear to slow the vehicle
Metal spike strip can drop from rear of vehicle

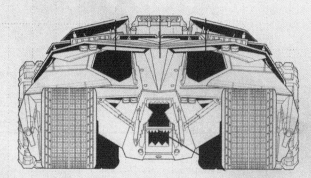

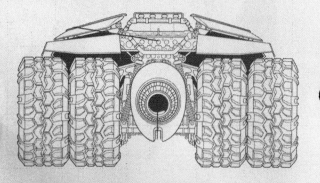

COCKPIT DETAILS

3-D hologram generator and one-touch controls
High-definition monitors give multi-angle views of pursuers
Bulletproof glass
Air filters for chemical attack
GPS (global positioning system) includes thorough maps of Gotham's streets
Voice recognition
Radio communication
"Loiter" setting utilizes a "ghost driver" to give the appearance of activity

THE BAT-POD

The Batmobile's cockpit mechanism can eject a fully functioning motorcycle. This Bat-Pod has a sleek design that gives it the ability to pivot up walls and navigate easily through tight situations.

To drive it, I have to lie on my stomach and guide the Bat-Pod with my body weight.

AYNE ENTERPRISES

APPLIED SCIENCES DIVISION

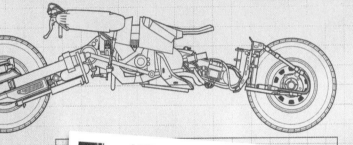

EXTERNAL DETAILS

Anti-aircraft gun mounted on wheels
No external exhaust, the engine/chassis
  is the exhaust system
Radiator doubles as foot pads
Protective arm shields on handle bars
Bat-Pod has two engines, one in hub on
  front wheel and the other in back wheel
EMP rifle mount

SPECS

WEIGHT: 1,500 pounds
LENGTH: 8 feet
WIDTH: 3 feet
HEIGHT: 3 feet, 6 inches

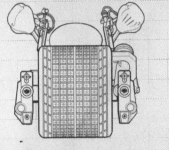

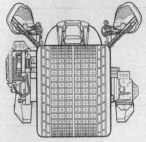

THE BAT

The Bat is a mobile flying vehicle capable of handling tight maneuvers around and between Gotham's buildings and skyscrapers. Dual propellers on the underside of the aircraft create a vortex that lifts the vehicle straight up into the air. These spinning blades are so powerful that they can knock down bystanders. The Bat's autopilot feature allows it to hover quietly, enabling me to stay hidden in the city's toughest neighborhoods.

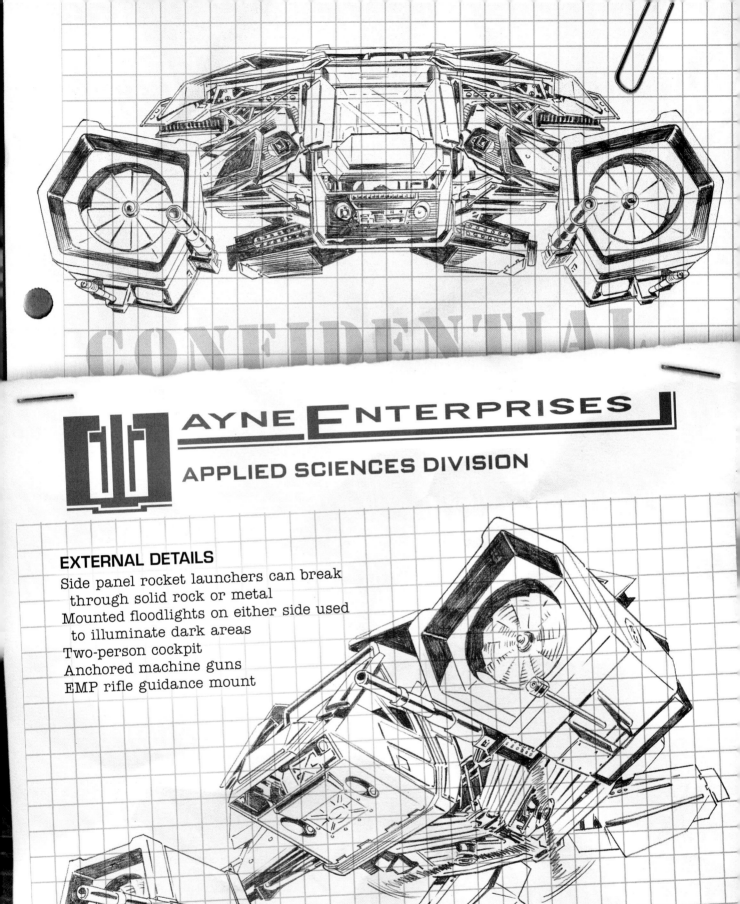

AYNE ENTERPRISES

APPLIED SCIENCES DIVISION

EXTERNAL DETAILS

Side panel rocket launchers can break
  through solid rock or metal
Mounted floodlights on either side used
  to illuminate dark areas
Two-person cockpit
Anchored machine guns
EMP rifle guidance mount

BANE

Little is known about Bane. He was born in prison and trained in the darkest forms of deception by the League of Shadows, but rumor has it he was cast out due to his extreme behavior.

Bane is a ferocious hand-to-hand fighter who is willing to do anything in order to take down his opponents.

Bane is in peak physical shape, but he must wear a breathing apparatus that feeds him pain-relieving gas due to an old injury.

He's never been photographed without his mask and only a handful of people have seen his face.

While his true motives remain a mystery, he appears to be building an army of followers in the dark tunnels underneath Gotham in order to create his own League of Shadows.

CATWOMAN/SELINA KYLE

Selina Kyle is a world-class cat burglar and mistress of disguise. She's cunning and devious, but I've noticed she has a deep sense of honor. As Catwoman, she targets Gotham's wealthiest.

Her weapons usually include infrared goggles, bladed high-heel boots, and a belt filled with lock picks.

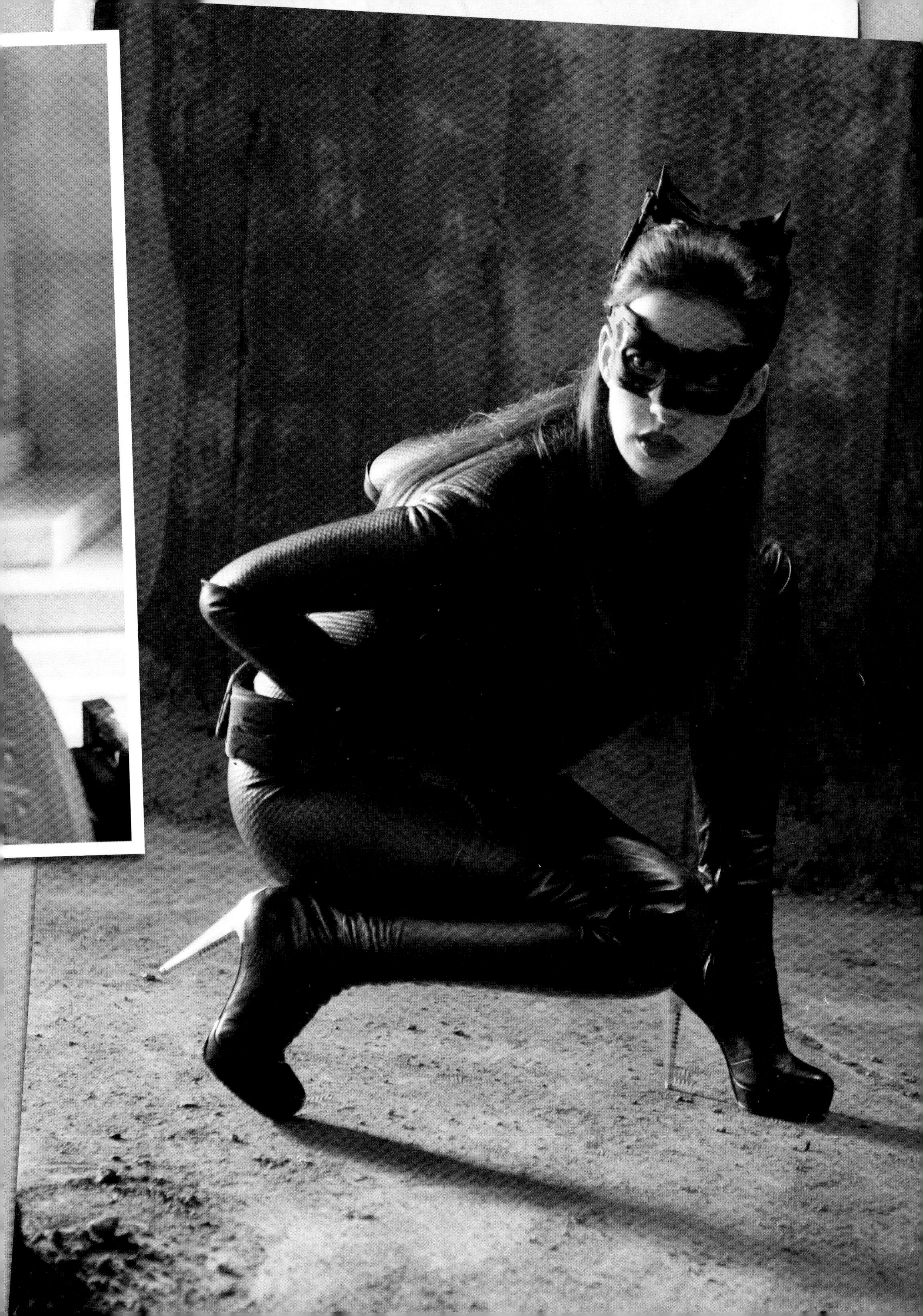

RĀ's al GHŪL

Rā's al Ghūl was the leader of a secret society of assassins known as the League of Shadows. Rā's trained his fighters in a variety of martial arts and deployed them around the world in an effort to destroy society from within so that it could be rebuilt in his image. Rā's controlled League operations from a monastery hidden away in the Himalayan Mountains, but his evil presence was felt throughout the globe. Prior to his death, it was rumored that Rā's was immortal and had lived for centuries.

His name translates to "Head of the Demon" in Arabic.

During my training with the League of Shadows, I worked with Henri Ducard, a master of martial arts. Ducard tested me both mentally and physically. He broke my spirit and questioned my courage in battle. He believed that symbolism and deception were important tools in an arsenal.

Ducard helped me to master my own fears, and I hoped to return to Gotham and use his teachings in my battle against injustice. We clashed when I refused to take a man's life, and I left the League of Shadows forever. Ducard later revealed the greatest deception of all—he was actually the great Rā's al Ghūl himself.

THE JOKER

The Joker is one of the most dangerous and unpredictable adversaries I've ever encountered. His origins are shrouded in mystery, but what we do know is that wherever he is, violence and chaos follow.

His motives are unknown, but he enjoys making fools out of the people of Gotham City.

The maniacal Joker plays by his own set of rules and has a complete disregard for human life. The Joker employs many criminals to help him carry out his elaborate evil plans.

He often makes his cronies wear clown masks while his own scarred face and stark white makeup serve to scare his already frightened victims.

The Joker enjoys using big explosions and other theatrical weapons to get the city's attention.

CARMINE FALCONE

Carmine Falcone was once the head of Gotham's most notorious crime family. Falcone delighted in corrupting the good people of the city and often blackmailed Gotham's best police officers into working for him. As Batman, I made it my mission to see Falcone's empire destroyed in order to restore Gotham to its former glory.

As the city's biggest thug, Falcone had an army of hit men at his disposal led by Salvatore "Boss" Maroni.

THE SCARECROW/JONATHAN CRANE

Doctor Jonathan Crane was the head of Arkham Asylum until he began dabbling in crime as the fearmongering Scarecrow. With the backing of mob boss Carmine Falcone, Crane brought a powerful mind-bending drug into Gotham and used it to develop a toxin that gives life to a person's worst fears.

Wearing a scarecrow costume, Crane uses his fear gas to control people with his disturbed brand of psychological warfare.

ALFRED

Alfred Pennyworth is more than just a butler; he's been a trusted friend and a wise mentor since I was a young boy. Throughout my war on crime, Alfred has been assisting me.

On more than a few occasions, his medical knowledge has been invaluable. His calm presence and wise words have kept me going. Alfred hasn't always supported my actions as Batman, but he always fights for justice.

LUCIUS FOX

Lucius Fox is the brains behind Applied Sciences, the Research and Development wing of Wayne Enterprises. Here Lucius developed many technological marvels, some of which had to be shelved.

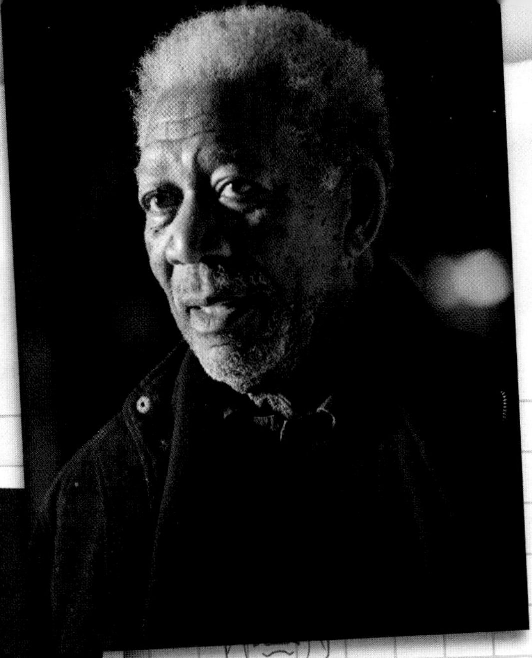

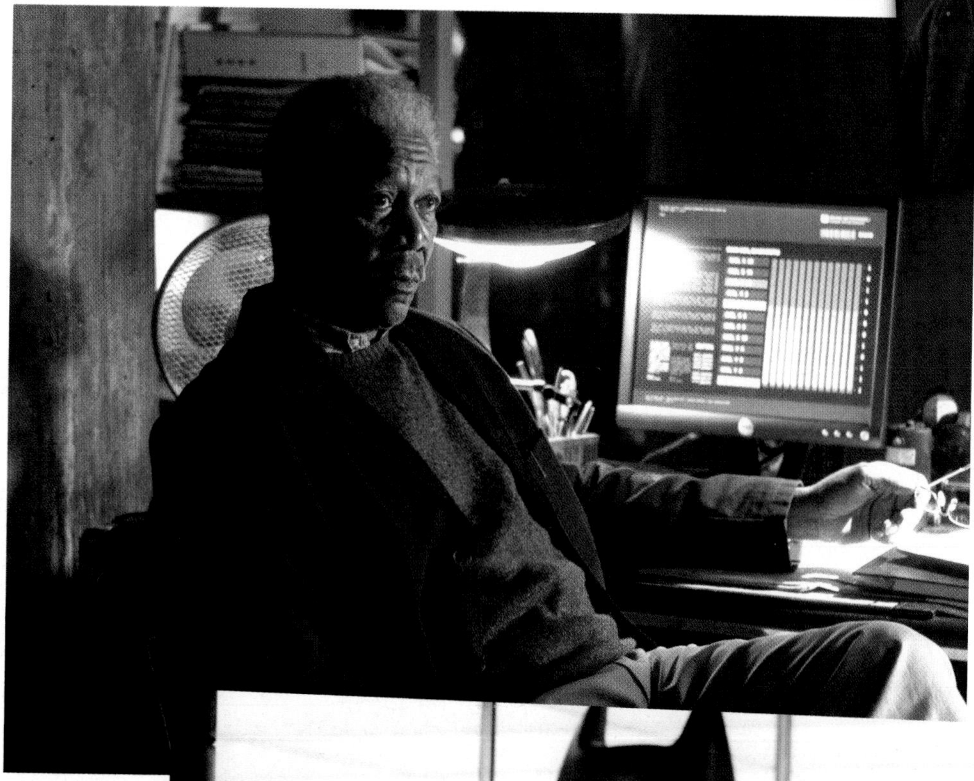

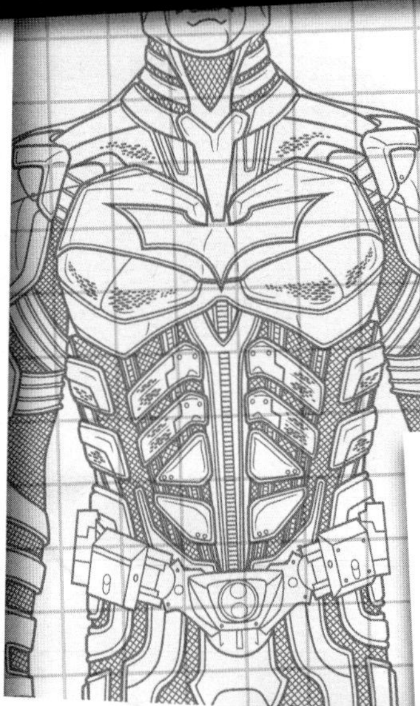

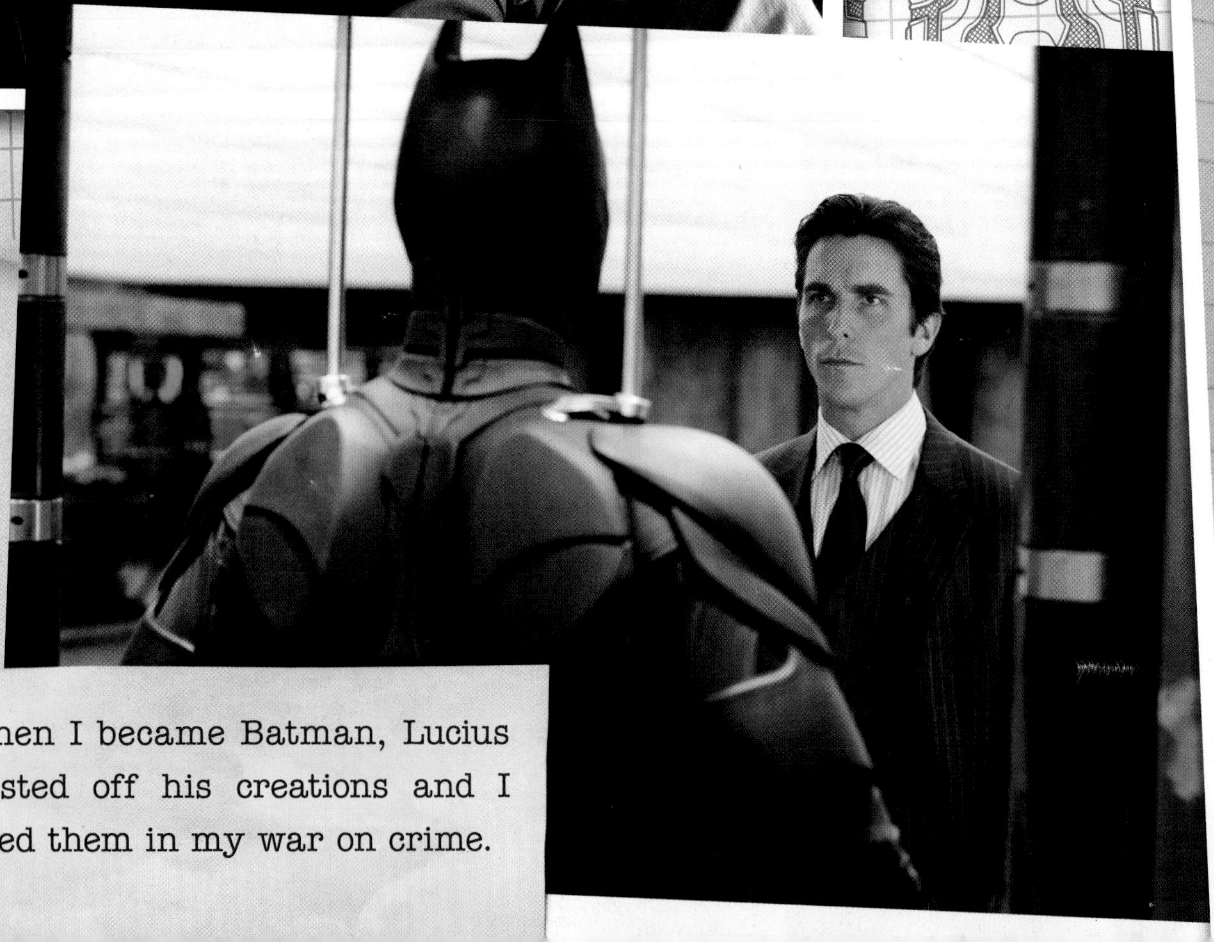

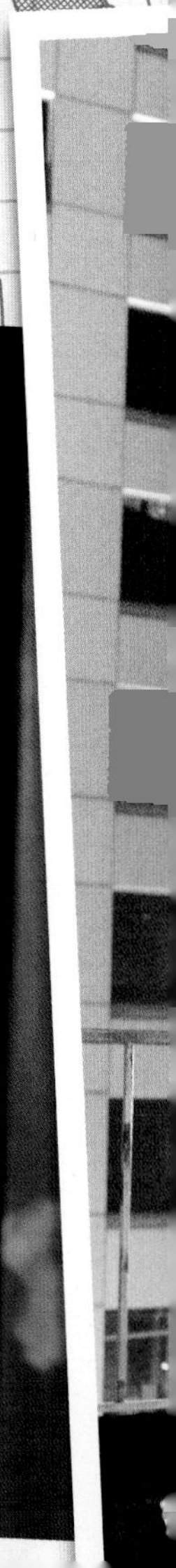

When I became Batman, Lucius dusted off his creations and I used them in my war on crime.

JAMES GORDON

When I began my career as Batman, the criminals had taken over the city and much of the Gotham City Police Department. One smart and sharp lieutenant stood out with his strong morals and sense of justice—James "Jim" Gordon. He is now commissioner, and his leadership has changed Gotham City for the better.

Gordon's honor and courage have made him a trusted partner.

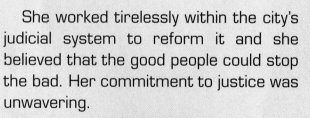

RACHEL DAWES

Rachel Dawes was one of my closest childhood friends. As an adult, she became one of the savviest litigators in Gotham.

She worked tirelessly within the city's judicial system to reform it and she believed that the good people could stop the bad. Her commitment to justice was unwavering.

Rachel knew the risks in challenging the city's criminals, and in the end she lost her life during the Joker's rampage.

JOHN BLAKE

John Blake is a passionate young police officer who shares my vision of a crime-free Gotham City. Blake quickly formed a strong bond with Jim Gordon and has learned a great deal under his guidance.

MIRANDA TATE

As a board member of Wayne Enterprises, Miranda Tate helped me resume my father's philanthropic endeavors. She is also is a very clever and intelligent businesswoman.

HARVEY DENT

There was a time when I called Harvey Dent a friend. As Gotham's District Attorney, he was an unstoppable crusader for justice. His passion and charisma took the city by storm, and he put away many high-profile gangsters. Harvey realized that in order to achieve his goals, he would need my help. He became Gotham's ray of light and a symbol of hope to the people.

Harvey Dent's mind was split in two by one of the Joker's violent pranks.

The once-proud defender of justice quickly descended into madness. Half of his face became scarred—just like the lucky coin his father gave him. Harvey embraced the nickname Two-Face and set about getting his revenge. Harvey tragically lost his life, and his brief criminal career is now one of Gotham's biggest secrets.

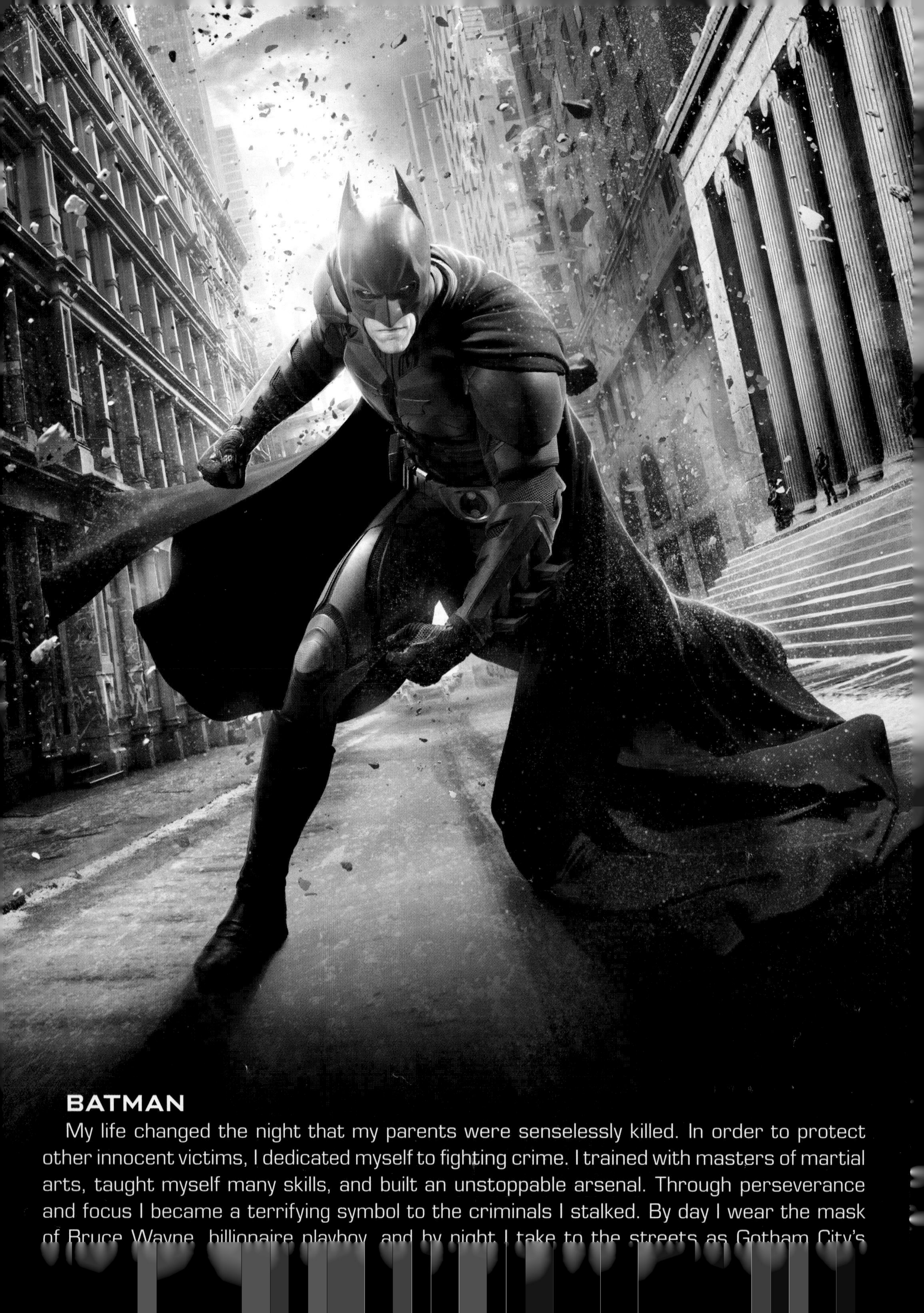

BATMAN

My life changed the night that my parents were senselessly killed. In order to protect other innocent victims, I dedicated myself to fighting crime. I trained with masters of martial arts, taught myself many skills, and built an unstoppable arsenal. Through perseverance and focus I became a terrifying symbol to the criminals I stalked. By day I wear the mask of Bruce Wayne, billionaire playboy, and by night I take to the streets as Gotham City's